The Three Bears in the Ministry

A FAITH TALE

Story Retold by BEVERLY CAPPS BURGESS

Illustrations by ELIZABETH LINDER

A Little Castle Book

the Little Castle

Harrison House

Unless otherwise indicated,
all Scripture quotations are taken from
the *King James Version* of the Bible.

6th Printing
Over 70,000 in Print

The Three Bears in the Ministry
ISBN 0-89274-252-6

P. O. Box 188
England, Arkansas 72046

Published by Harrison House, Inc.
P. O. Box 35035
Tulsa, Oklahoma 74153

Printed in the United States of America.

The Three Bears in the Ministry

A Faith Tale

Once upon a time, there were three bears: Mama Bear, Papa Bear, and Baby Bear. They were very happy because upon Jesus they had cast every care.

Casting all your care upon him; for he careth for you.
1 Peter 5:7

Papa Bear was called to be an evangelist. All day they had been out preaching. They came home praising God and singing.

Make a joyful noise unto God, all ye lands: Sing forth the honour of his name: make his praise glorious.

Psalm 66:1,2

As the bears walked in, they knew someone was in the house. But they were not afraid. Papa Bear told Baby Bear, ''Be quiet as a mouse.''

Fear thou not; for I am with thee: be not dismayed; for I am thy God: I will strengthen thee; yea, I will help thee; yea, I will uphold thee with the right hand of my righteousness.
Isaiah 41:10

Born Again

Mama Bear found Goldilocks asleep in Baby Bear's bed. Papa Bear prayed in the Spirit to know what to do. Then he awoke Goldilocks and gently said . . .

Likewise the Spirit also helpeth our infirmities: for we know not what we should pray for as we ought: but the Spirit itself maketh intercession for us with groanings which cannot be uttered.

And he that searcheth the hearts knoweth what is the mind of the Spirit, because he maketh intercession for the saints according to the will of God.

Romans 8:26,27

JESUS
LOVES
ME!

"Honey, the Lord told me that you've run away. God loves you very much. He wants you to be born again today!"

. . . Except a man be born again, he cannot see the kingdom of God.

John 3:3

Goldilocks began to cry, ''I ran away because I was so mad. I really do love my Mom and my Dad. Tell me how to make Jesus my Lord. I feel so very bad.''

Children, obey your parents in the Lord: for this is right.
Ephesians 6:1

Mama Bear opened her Bible and read Romans 10:9,10. Baby Bear explained to Goldilocks how Jesus died for her sin.

If thou shalt confess with thy mouth the Lord Jesus, and shalt believe in thine heart that God hath raised him from the dead, thou shalt be saved.

Romans 10:9,10

Goldilocks prayed and asked forgiveness for her unbelief. She confessed Jesus as Lord and believed God that His promises He will keep.

And when he is come, he will reprove the world of sin, and of righteousness, and of judgment.

John 16:8

Everyone was joyful. Papa Bear said, "Now that you are born again, you will need power. The Holy Spirit is given and is for this hour."

But ye shall receive power, after that the Holy Ghost is come upon you: and ye shall be witnesses unto me both in Jerusalem, and in all Judea, and in Samaria, and unto the uttermost part of the earth.

Acts 1:8

Papa Bear turned to Acts 2:4. He read that scripture and several more. Mama Bear and Baby Bear prayed in the Spirit quietly, while sitting on the floor.

And they were all filled with the Holy Ghost, and began to speak with other tongues, as the Spirit gave them utterance.
Acts 2:4

Papa Bear laid hands on Goldilocks and said, ''Receive ye the Holy Spirit.'' Goldilocks raised her hands and began to speak in other tongues where everyone could hear it.

Thus will I bless thee while I live: I will lift up my hands in thy name.

Psalm 63:4

When through praying, Goldilocks thought twice. She exclaimed, "I have to go tell my parents I'm a new creature in Christ."

Therefore if any man be in Christ, he is a new creature: old things are passed away; behold, all things are become new.
2 Corinthians 5:17

The three Bears took Goldilocks home in their car. She was ready to minister to her parents and was so glad it wasn't very far.

Whosoever therefore shall confess me before men, him will I confess also before my Father which is in heaven.

Matthew 10:32

PTL

When they arrived, Goldilocks gave her testimony of what the Lord had done. Right then, her family was born again and filled with the Holy Spirit—each and every one!

And all things are of God, who hath reconciled us to himself by Jesus Christ, and hath given to us the ministry of reconciliation.

2 Corinthians 5:18

PTL

HARRISON HOUSE
P. O. Box 35035 • Tulsa, OK 74153

Dear Friend,

As a believer and a responsible parent, it is so important for you to fill your child with God's Word. Our goal in this book is to engraft the Word of God into the child by applying the Word in a story that has been passed down for years. Your child will be able to see by example how to minister effectively and how to apply the Word in his or her own life.

The Scripture references on each page help you to relate the story and illustrations to the biblical principles you desire to develop in your child. Be faithful in reading and training your child in God's Word!

In Him,
Bill and Beverly Burgess